CRITICAL THINKING
IN
AMERICAN HISTORY™

Analyzing the Boston Tea Party

Establishing Cause-and-Effect Relationships

Greg Roza

rosen
central™

The Rosen Publishing Group, Inc., New York

For Lincoln

Published in 2006 by The Rosen Publishing Group, Inc.
29 East 21st Street, New York, NY 10010

Copyright © 2006 by The Rosen Publishing Group, Inc.

First Edition   APR 26 2006

Library of Congress Cataloging-in-Publication Data

Roza, Greg.
Analyzing the Boston Tea Party: establishing cause-and-effect relationships/
Greg Roza.—1st ed.
    p. cm.—(Critical thinking in American history)
Includes index.
ISBN 1-4042-0411-3 (library binding)
1. Boston Tea Party, 1773—Juvenile literature. 2. Boston Tea Party,
1773—Study and teaching (Secondary)—Juvenile literature. 3. United
States—History—Colonial period, ca. 1600–1775—Juvenile literature.
4. United States—History—Colonial period, ca. 1600–1775—Study and
teaching (Secondary)—Juvenile literature.
I. Title. II. Series.
E215.7.R698 2006
973.3'115—dc22

                                                            2005001393

Manufactured in the United States of America

On the cover: A postcard (*left*) from 1910 depicts colonists disguised as Native Americans about to throw a box of tea into Boston Harbor in 1773. A print (*right*) from 1770 depicts fighting during the Boston Massacre.

Contents

Independence in the Colonies

By the late 1600s, several European countries, including England, France, and Spain, had established colonies in North America. Many early settlements were nothing more than barricaded forts where Europeans traded with Native Americans for goods, especially the animal furs that were popular in Europe. English and French fur traders established alliances with the Native Americans with whom they traded. Many of these alliances lasted well into the 1700s.

A vast ocean separated the colonies from England. Most colonists had faced great hardships to create a life for themselves in the wilderness. Although they proudly considered themselves British citizens, they had also developed a strong sense of independence. They were satisfied in their ability to survive and flourish. As more people

Word Works

✓ **alliance** A close association formed between people or groups of people to reach a common objective. An "ally" is someone with whom you have formed a positive relationship.

✓ **animosity** Bad feelings between two parties that often result in fighting or violence.

✓ **industry** A group of productive or profitable businesses.

✓ **rebellion** Opposition to authority.

In the beginning, trade between Native Americans and Europeans benefitted both parties. Indians were eager to offer animal skins in exchange for highly prized metal hardware and cloth.

traveled to the New World to seek fortune and adventure, the tiny settlements grew into towns. By the early 1700s, the British colonists had established their own farms and industries. They developed their own governments and laws, and British laws often had little meaning to them. It was this sense of independence that would eventually cause animosity between them and the leaders of England, ultimately resulting in outbreaks of rebellion such as the Boston Tea Party.

The French and Indian Wars

The French and Indian Wars were four wars between France and England fought from 1689 to 1763. These wars included King William's War (1689–1697); Queen Anne's War (1702–1713); King George's War (1744–1748); and the French and Indian War (1754–1763), which was known as the Nine Years' War in Europe and Canada, but the Seven Years' War in the United States.

During these four wars, both sides aligned themselves with different Native American tribes that helped them fight their enemy. France and England fought for control of the fur trade, for the land between the Appalachian Mountains and the Mississippi River, and for fishing rights off the shores of modern-day Newfoundland.

At the end of the French and Indian Wars, England controlled nearly all of the land between the Atlantic Ocean and the Mississippi River, including Canada. Spain, which had helped France attack southern British settlements during Queen Anne's War, also lost the area today known as Florida to the British. Most colonists took pride in being part of the most powerful country in the world, but they still valued their independence in America. England, however, thought of the American colonies as its children. It also thought that it was about time the colonies helped financially support the British Empire.

Get Graphic

Conflict	Years	European Struggle	Outcome	Result
King William's War	1689 to 1697	War of the League of Augsburg	draw	The Treaty of Ryswick returned the land France and England had lost during the war.
Queen Anne's War	1702 to 1713	War of the Spanish Succession	England wins	The Treaty of Utrecht gave Nova Scotia, Newfoundland, and the territory around Hudson Bay to England.
King George's War	1744 to 1748	War of the Austrian Succession	draw	The Treaty of Aix-la-Chapelle returned the land France and England had lost during the war.
The French and Indian War	1754 to 1763	War first broke out in America, then spread to Europe (the Seven Years' War [1756–1763])	England wins	The Treaty of Paris granted England France's land in Canada, land east of the Mississippi River, and the Spanish area that is today Florida; France gave New Orleans and land west of the Mississippi to Spain.

✓ Out of which European struggle did King William's War grow?

✓ Which treaty ended King George's War?

✓ In what year did the Seven Years' War begin?

✓ What were the results of the French and Indian War?

The Proclamation of 1763

Prior to and during the French and Indian Wars, the land west of the Appalachian Mountains was reserved for Native Americans. Treaties prohibited colonists from settling on these lands. After England won the French and Indian Wars, however, colonists began crossing into and settling the Indian Territory. Many colonists hoped to profit from the land and resources of the western frontier. Native Americans resented the colonists invading their hunting grounds. In the spring of 1763, an Ottawa chief named Pontiac led attacks on British colonists living in the western frontier. Hundreds of colonists died in the attacks. King George III and the British parliament feared the confrontation would lead to a war with the Native Americans. England could not afford to go to war at that time, so it passed the Proclamation of 1763. This

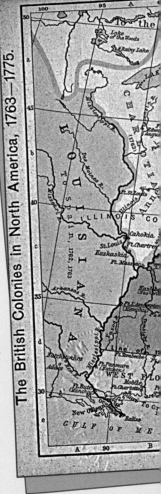

The British Colonies in North America, 1763–1775.

Fact Finders

Use the map at right to answer the questions below.

✓ What river formed the western boundary of the Indian Territory?

✓ What country owned the land to the west of the Indian Territory?

✓ Name the states that did not border the Indian Territories.

This map details the region of America under British colonial control between 1763 and 1775. Although British parliament issued the Proclamation of 1763 to keep European colonists from encroaching upon Indian lands, the colonists did little to follow the new rule.

document prohibited colonial settlement of the Native American lands west of the Appalachian Mountains. Britain sent troops to guard the border to the western frontier and keep the colonists out. Many colonists were angry about the Proclamation of 1763. They felt England had no right to prohibit them from settling on frontier lands. They were also offended by the presence of British soldiers in their towns.

War Debt

Despite winning the French and Indian Wars, England was on shaky financial ground in 1763. In funding the wars, its national debt had nearly doubled. King George III told members of Parliament to find a way to pay off this debt. The British parliament began passing laws designed to raise colonial money to help increase England's funds. Most members of Parliament did not expect colonists to pay off the debt directly. They did, however, expect the colonies to pay taxes to fund the British troops guarding the western frontier.

Colonists had grown accustomed to a sense of freedom they had attained living so far away from England. They already paid their own local taxes, much of which had been used to fund the British wars in America. The colonies received no representation in the British parliament, and, therefore, believed they could not be governed by laws created by Parliament. In the years after the French and

Q & A

Write a short answer to each of the questions below on a sheet of paper. Then meet with a small group of classmates to discuss your responses. Did everyone have similar answers? Were there disagreements between you and your classmates?

✓ Do you think it was fair of the British parliament to expect the colonists to pay a tax to fund the troops guarding the western frontier?

✓ Should the British parliament have only allowed the colonists to continue taxing themselves?

✓ Was it fair to tax the colonists without giving them a voice in Parliament?

In this illustration, King George III passes through London. While the British may have been opposed to higher taxes under the king, colonists in America felt that it was unfair to be forced to pay taxes without being represented in Parliament.

Indian Wars, "taxation without representation is tyranny" became a slogan that echoed ominously throughout the colonies. It was this idea that eventually led to the Boston Tea Party—an open act of rebellion that helped convince the colonies that war with England was the only path to total independence.

The Sugar and Quartering Acts

King George's chief cabinet minister was a man named George Grenville. Grenville and King George thought it was about time the colonists began to contribute to the wealth of the British Empire. They also wanted to demonstrate their power over the colonies.

Grenville's first move was to establish the Revenue Act of 1764, which was also called the Sugar Act. The Sugar Act placed a three-cent tax on each gallon of molasses coming into the colonies from locations outside the British Empire. This law also gave British authorities permission to search the homes of people under suspicion of violating the law. Colonial industries that were dependent on sugar, especially the rum-making industry, complained that the tax would take too much of their profits. They threatened to boycott British goods. In 1766, the tax was reduced to one penny per gallon.

Word Works

✓ **boycott** To refuse to do business with a company or person in an attempt to make them change their business practices.

✓ **cabinet** The group of chief advisers to a king or president.

✓ **quarter** To provide with shelter.

✓ **revenue** The income produced by a given source, such as a tax.

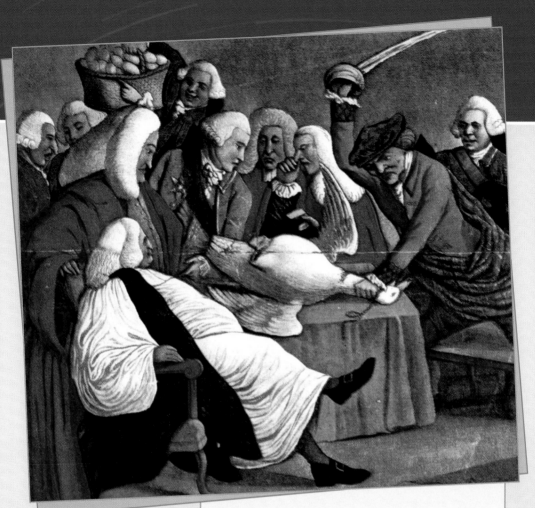

This political cartoon, a visual play on the phrase "the goose that laid the golden eggs," appeared in British newspapers in the 1770s. The goose was a symbol representing the colonies. The cartoonist was emphasizing the foolishness of Parliament overtaxing its colonists since trade between them was already so valuable.

In 1765, the British parliament passed the Quartering Act. This was an attempt to make the colonists pay for the British troops stationed in the colonies. The Quartering Act ordered the colonists to provide living quarters and supplies for British soldiers. Most colonists obeyed the Quartering Act but were unhappy about having to share their personal things with British soldiers.

The Stamp Act

In 1765, Grenville and the British parliament passed the Stamp Act. Like the Sugar and Quartering Acts, the Stamp Act was designed to raise money for British troops stationed in the colonies. The Stamp Act called for a tax on most kinds of paper in use in the colonies, from deeds and documents to newspapers and playing cards. In accordance with the law, all paper goods were printed on paper bearing an official stamp.

While colonists were unhappy about the Sugar and Quartering Acts, the Stamp Act provoked more dissent. Violent uprisings in many colonies were now more common. Most colonists were angered that the British parliament would tax the

Think Tank

Samuel Adams was one of the colonies' loudest voices in the struggle for independence. When the British parliament issued the Stamp Act, Adams helped to unite the colonists in their fight against taxation without representation. After the Stamp Act was passed, Adams said, "If our trade be taxed, why not our lands or produce, in short, everything we possess? They tax us without having legal representation."

✓ Divide the class into several small groups.

✓ Create a poster that notifies citizens of the Stamp Act Congress. Include the following elements: the quote by Samuel Adams, meeting date and location, and a graphic that displays the main idea of your poster.

✓ Display the posters in the classroom and have all the groups reassemble to discuss them as a class. Whose poster would have been most effective in gaining support for the Stamp Act Congress?

This engraving shows colonists engaged in what became known as the Stamp Act riots in Boston on August 25, 1765. Colonial opposition to the law was so strong that when it was implemented there were no tax collectors available for hire.

colonies so heavily without giving them a voice in Parliament. Organized groups of colonists protested the law and boycotted British goods. Some colonial assemblies passed resolutions condemning the Stamp Act. The Massachusetts House of Representatives invited delegates from each of the colonies to attend a formal meeting to discuss the issue. The Stamp Act Congress met in New York in October 1765, and this was the first united colonial protest against the British. The congress decided that taxes could not be collected without the consent of the citizens. As a result, the British parliament repealed the Stamp Act in 1766.

The Townshend Acts

The majority of people living in the colonies saw the Sugar, Quartering, and Stamp Acts as a threat to their independence. The British parliament still considered itself the "parent," and the colonies were its "children."

In 1767, Parliament reduced the British land tax. To make up for the loss in tax money, it passed the Townshend Acts, named after the parliamentary treasurer, Charles Townshend. These acts placed indirect taxes called duties on many imported goods, including glass, lead, paint, paper, and tea. It also set up a customs house in Boston to collect the duties. The money collected was used to pay the salaries of British colonial officials. This made them independent of colonial lawmakers, and more inclined to enforce British laws.

Townshend thought he could fool the colonists into accepting taxes by masking them as duties. The colonists were not fooled. Many responded with

Fact Finders

Look for the answers to these questions as you read the text.

✓ Parliament passed the Townshend Acts to make up for the reduction of what British tax?

✓ For whom were the Townshend Acts named?

✓ How did colonists respond to the Townshend Acts?

✓ In what year were the Townshend Acts repealed?

Known as the Old South Meeting House, this building, erected in 1729, was originally a Puritan church. Just before the Boston Tea Party, about 5,000 colonists met here to protest the tea tax on December 16, 1773.

petitions, boycotts, and violence. In 1770, Parliament repealed all of the Townshend Acts except for the duty on tea. It kept this duty to assert its right to tax the colonies.

The Boston Massacre

Anger over British taxes resulted in more protests in the colonies. On March 5, 1770, a group of colonists began taunting a British sentry (guard) in front of the customs house. As more and more colonists joined the scene, the sentry signaled for help. Soon an armed group of seven or eight soldiers, led by Captain Thomas Preston, was surrounded by a mob of about 400 angry colonists.

Accounts of what happened next differ. Some colonists claimed that Preston ordered his men to fire into the crowd. During his trial, after which he was acquitted of any wrong-doing, Captain Preston claimed that even though the colonists hit the soldiers with snow-balls and

Paper Works

✓ The engraving shown here, *The Bloody Massacre Perpetrated in King Street* (1770), was made and sold by Boston silversmith Paul Revere. The depiction of the event has been proven to be inaccurate. However, Revere consciously used his engraving to rally colonists against Britain.

✓ Revere's engraving is one example of patriot propaganda. It presents the event in a light that makes the British role appear worse than it probably was and the colonists' role more innocent that it probably was.

✓ Write an essay explaining how propaganda like Revere's engraving affected the thinking of American colonists. Explain how it shaped the events leading up to the American Revolution. In conclusion, state whether you think it was right or wrong of patriots to spread propaganda like this, and tell why.

Angry colonists depicted in this engraving surround British soldiers in front of the customs house in Boston on March 5, 1770. After the soldiers opened fire, killing five colonists including Crispus Attucks, the event became known as the Boston Massacre.

clubs, he ordered them not to fire on the crowd. His soldiers fired in fear, and he reprimanded them for disobeying his orders. Regardless of who was correct, six people were injured and five people died in the violence.

The event was soon dubbed the "Boston Massacre," a phrase coined by Samuel Adams. Exaggerated news of the conflict spread quickly thanks to patriot propaganda. It was presented as proof of British tyranny over the colonies. Public opinion began to turn against England. This event marked a major turn toward the desire for revolution in the colonies.

The Tea Act

Despite the rising violence and negative feelings toward the British, Parliament still searched for ways to demonstrate its dominance over the colonies. Once again, it attempted to use its legislative powers to control the lives of the colonists and raise money for the British Empire.

Tea was a valued staple in colonial America. To avoid paying the Townshend duty on tea, colonists had begun smuggling tea from the Netherlands into the colonies. Britain's East India Company had been the main source for colonial tea before the Townshend Acts. The company had millions of pounds of unsold tea,

Fact Finders

Look for the answers to the following questions as you read the text.

✓ What does "legislative" mean?

✓ How did colonists avoid paying the British duty on tea?

✓ Which company had been the main source of colonial tea before the Townshend Acts?

✓ For what reasons were the colonists against the Tea Act?

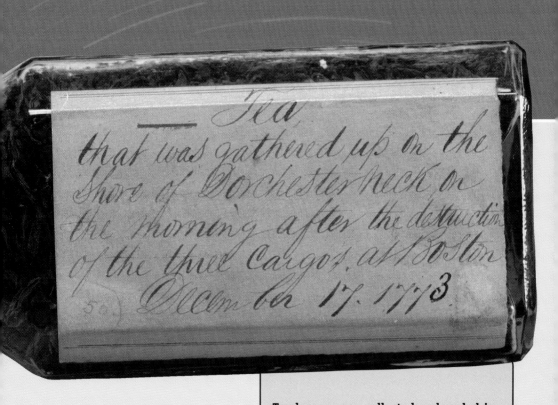

Tea, that was gathered up on the Shore of Dorchester neck, on the morning after the destruction of the three Cargos, at Boston December 17. 1773.

Tea leaves were collected and sealed in this glass bottle by T. M. Harris during the time of the Boston Tea Party, the colonial protest to the taxes levied upon colonists by the British parliament. It is now part of the collection of the Massachusetts Historical Society.

and it was struggling financially due to the business lost to smuggled tea. It asked Parliament for help. In response, Parliament passed the Tea Act in 1773. This law reduced the duty on tea brought into the colonies by the East India Company, allowing it to sell tea in the colonies more cheaply than ever before. The act also allowed the East India Company to sell the tea solely to pro-British merchants, which angered colonial businessmen. Parliament estimated that the colonists' fondness for tea would compel them to buy the cheaper tea. By doing this, they would finally be acknowledging England's right to tax them.

Colonial Anger

People in the colonies were repeatedly outraged over the actions of the British parliament. They saw through Parliament's thinly veiled attempts to assert its right to tax the colonies. In addition, by passing the Tea Act, Parliament had aided the East India Company in establishing a monopoly on the tea trade in order to avoid bankruptcy. This angered local merchants who would lose money. Colonists' anger often resulted in violence against British tax collectors. Some collectors were even tarred and feathered, and then forced out of town.

In many ports, the agents who were selected to sell the East India Company tea were compelled by an angry public to resign before the tea even arrived. When East India Company ships showed up in New York and Philadelphia loaded with tea, colonial leaders would not allow the ships to dock, and they were forced to turn back. In Charleston, West Virginia, colonial leaders ordered the incoming tea to be stored in warehouses, where much of it

Word Works

✓ **bankrupt** Reduced to a state of financial ruin.

✓ **monopoly** Exclusive possession or control of a good or service.

✓ **resign** Quit.

✓ **tar and feather** To cover someone with tar and feathers in order to humiliate and punish him or her.

In this British illustration from 1774, a tax collector who has been tarred and feathered is being forced to drink tea. During the colonial protests against the Stamp Act, the colonists' anger grew stronger against Parliament. Fewer men stepped forward to collect taxes for England. In the background, men can be seen dumping tea in Boston Harbor.

rotted. In Boston, however, the tea ships were allowed to dock. The citizens of Boston knew that if the tea was allowed to be unloaded, they would have taken one step back in their fight against British tyranny.

Confrontation in Boston

The East India Company tea agents in Boston were the sons and nephew of the Boston governor and British official Thomas Hutchinson. His family stood to make a great deal of money as part of the East India Company tea monopoly. On November 27, 1773, the *Dartmouth* arrived in Boston Harbor loaded with East India Company tea. Two days later the *Beaver* and the *Eleanor* also arrived with their cargo of tea. Despite warnings from other agents, Hutchinson refused to send the ships away as other colonial ports had done.

The Sons of Liberty, a patriotic society in Boston, was determined to win the fight against British taxes. Members of the Sons of Liberty, including their vocal leader Samuel Adams, angrily patrolled the port, ensuring that the three ships did not unload their cargo. Hutchinson and his relatives still refused to send the ships away. They insisted that the tea would be

Q & A

Team up with a partner and take turns asking and answering the following questions. How are your answers different, and how are they the same?

✓ For what reasons do you think Thomas Hutchinson refused to send the ships away from Boston?

✓ Do you think Samuel Adams and the Sons of Liberty were right in obstructing the ships' crews from unloading their cargo? Why or why not?

✓ What do you think the Sons of Liberty was hoping to achieve by protesting?

unloaded, brought ashore, and properly taxed according to the law. The colonists knew that if they were allowed to do that, then the British parliament would have accomplished what it had set out to do all along: assert its right to tax the colonies. The Sons of Liberty stubbornly refused to let the ships unload the tea.

This colonial broadside was published in Pennsylvania in 1773 to warn colonists against the evils of the East India Company. It states, "The East India Company will leave no stone unturned to become your masters. They themselves are well versed in tyranny, plunder, oppression, and bloodshed."

Boiling Point

In the end, the passing of the Tea Act was the event that steered the colonies down the inevitable course to revolution. According to the Tea Act, the tax on tea needed to be collected within twenty days of the ships arriving at port. This made December 16 the deadline for the collection of the tax on the tea that had arrived in Boston Harbor on November 27. Patriot Samuel Adams kept colonial anger high by staging frequent speeches at a nearby meetinghouse. At times, more than 5,000 colonists crowded into the port area to join the protest.

On December 16, both sides were still arguing about what to do with the tea. The owner of the *Dartmouth* agreed to

Fact Finders

Look for the answers to these questions as you read or reread the text.

✓ According to the Tea Act, the tax on tea needed to be collected within how many days upon its reaching port?

✓ What was the last day that the tax on the tea in Boston Harbor could be collected?

✓ Why was the captain of the *Dartmouth* unable to sail his ship out of Boston Harbor on December 16?

In this illustration, colonists toss boxes of tea into Boston Harbor. Just before the fateful evening, patriots had left Boston's Old South Meeting House, where many cried out, "Let every man do his duty and be true to his country."

take his ship back to England. However, British warships had been positioned just outside of Boston Harbor, prohibiting the *Dartmouth* from leaving port. British officials announced that the next day, December 17, they would seize the ships for nonpayment of the tea tax. The tea would then be made available for sale. The owner of the *Dartmouth* explained his predicament to a group of patriots at the Old South Meeting House. Samuel Adams and the Sons of Liberty knew they had to act now or bow to the will of the British parliament.

The Boston Tea Party

Samuel Adams knew this was the time for action. On his signal, about 150 members of the Sons of Liberty, dressed as Mohawk Indians, left the meetinghouse. Quietly and determinedly, they marched to the docks two by two. They boarded the three ships while the citizens of Boston watched silently from the piers. They demanded the keys to the holds of the ships from the crew members on watch, and received them without a fight. The men brought the cargo of tea onto the deck. For the next three hours, the men broke open 342 chests with hatchets and threw the tea into Boston Harbor. They worked hastily, fearing that British officials would attempt to stop them.

Think Tank

✓ Discuss the elements of a well-written newspaper article with the class. (For example, it should contain information on who, what, where, when, why, and how.) Also discuss letters to the editor, and what place, if any, personal opinion has in newspaper writing.

✓ Write a mock newspaper article describing the events of the Boston Tea Party. Choose one of the following perspectives:

• A reporter who has interviewed several people (including bystanders, members of the Sons of Liberty, and British officials).

• An eyewitness who has written a letter to the editor (again, you could be a bystander, a member of the Sons of Liberty, or a British official).

✓ Read the articles aloud to the class, and then discuss their differences and similarities.

The event known as the Boston Tea Party continues to fascinate through the years due to the fearlessness displayed. As this postcard records, roughly 200 men disguised as Indians tossed boxes of East India Company tea into Boston Harbor.

Some colonists tried to stuff their pockets with the coveted tea. When caught, these few men were stripped of their coats, which were then thrown into the harbor. The men were kicked and struck as they fled through the crowd watching on the docks. When they were done, the Sons of Liberty members removed their shoes and shook them over the water to make sure they did not have any evidence on them when they left the ship. The colonists marched off the ship just as they had marched onto it, their "party" having ended.

George Hewes: Eyewitness to History

One of the men who joined the Sons of Liberty on the night of December 16, 1773, was a young Boston shoemaker named George Hewes. Hewes had also been present at the Boston Massacre and served in a militia during the American Revolution. In 1835, ninety-three-year-old Hewes was the last surviving member of the Boston Tea Party. Sixty-two years after the historic event, Hewes became somewhat of a celebrity. Hewes was dubbed a hero of the American Revolution, and became a symbol of American patriotism.

Hewes gave a few interviews in his later years, providing one of the only eyewitness accounts of the Boston Tea Party that we have today. His detailed account of that night is brief, but it depicts

Paper Work

✓ Choose one of the following people who were present during the Boston Tea Party:

- A member of the Sons of Liberty;

- A citizen of Boston watching from the piers;

- British official and governor of Boston, Thomas Hutchinson;

- A British soldier watching from a warship positioned just outside the harbor.

✓ Write a short description of the Boston Tea Party through the eyes of the person you have chosen. What opinion of the event would that person have, a positive or negative one? What emotions might that person have experienced? At the end of the description, have your chosen person estimate what effect the Boston Tea Party may have on the near future.

In this engraving, colonial governor Thomas Hutchinson is pictured escaping from local rioters after demanding stamp taxes from them. It was Hutchinson's refusal to return the British tea ships to Europe with their cargo that led to the Boston Tea Party.

the danger the Sons of Liberty encountered while carrying out its rebellious task. "In about three hours from the time we went on board, we had thus broken and thrown overboard every tea chest to be found in the ship, while those in the other ships were disposing of the tea in the same way, at the same time. We were surrounded by British armed ships, but no attempt was made to resist us."

Aftermath

News of the Boston Tea Party quickly spread throughout the colonies and worked to strengthen the convictions of many colonists. Loyalists, colonists who remained loyal to British rule, decried the Boston Tea Party as the act of criminals and called for legal action against the Sons of Liberty. Colonists who were against British taxation, now called patriots, applauded the Boston Tea Party as a necessary step to the road to independence. Patriots staged similar acts of rebellion in other ports along the Atlantic coast. Tensions ran higher than ever before in the colonies as the actions of both

Think Tank

✓ Divide the class into three equal groups: Loyalists, patriots, and a neutral party.

✓ Patriots and Loyalists: research the beliefs of your group at the time of the Boston Tea Party. Use the information in this book, other books, and on the Internet.

✓ Prepare a short speech that sums up how your group feels about the actions taken during the Boston Tea Party. After a spokesperson from both groups has had a chance to speak, engage in a debate attempting to convince the neutral group of your position.

✓ After the debate, the members of the neutral group should discuss the points raised by the Loyalists and the patriots, and then vote on which group has the best argument.

✓ After the vote, re-form as a single group and discuss the exercise. Has the exercise changed your mind about the Boston Tea Party?

John Lamb, leader of the New York chapter of the Sons of Liberty, speaks to fellow patriots at New York's City Hall concerning the landing of British ships containing East India tea in New York harbor in 1773. Lamb would later help patriots seize New York's customs house in protest.

Loyalists and patriots became more impassioned and at times violent.

The British response to the Boston Tea Party was swift and decisive. Parliament declared that Boston was in a state of rebellion, and immediately sent British troops to secure the city. King George III and Parliament were furious. They wanted to make an example of Boston for the rest of the colonies. They were hoping to squash similar outbreaks and warn the colonists against questioning the authority of British laws.

The Intolerable Acts

To punish the citizens of Boston, and to warn all colonists about the repercussions of challenging British authority, the British parliament passed five acts in 1774. The colonists called these acts the Intolerable or Coercive Acts. The Boston Port Act closed the port of Boston until the tea the patriots had dumped into the harbor was paid for, thus showing the British the respect they believed they deserved. The Massachusetts Government Act gave the governor full power to appoint all government officials and judges, taking those powers away from the people of Boston. The Administration of Justice Act declared that any British soldier or officer accused of murder would be sent to England for a trial.

A new Quartering Act was passed, requiring colonial citizens to clothe, feed, and house British soldiers and officers. The Quebec Act

Think Tank

✓ Divide the class into smaller groups.

✓ Within the small groups, discuss each of the five Intolerable Acts, as well as their effects on the colonists. Use these questions to guide your discussion: Why did colonists dub the acts "intolerable" and "coercive"? Which of the acts do you feel was the most damaging to the colonists and why? How important do you think the Intolerable Acts were in uniting the colonists against England?

✓ Select a spokesperson for your group. Reassemble as a large group and give each spokesperson a chance to explain his or her group's opinions. How were those opinions the same, and how were they different?

Quebec, 1774
Other British possessions
Indian territory
Spanish possessions

Hudson Bay

HUDSON'S BAY COMPANY

Lake Superior
QUEBEC 1774
Lake Ontario
Lake Michigan
Lake Huron
Lake Erie

Ohio River

LOUISIANA

INDIAN COUNTRY

ORIGINAL BRITISH COLONIES

ATLANTIC OCEAN

EAST FLORIDA

WEST FLORIDA

300 Miles
300 Kilometers

extended the border of Canada, south of the Ohio River, where many French citizens still lived. This angered British colonists who believed that land was theirs to settle.

Boston struggled financially under the Intolerable Acts but received aid from nearby cities. Boston leaders called for a meeting of colonial delegates to discuss the boycott of British goods. In the end, the Intolerable Acts helped unite the colonies in their fight against British control.

This map shows the extent of British possessions along the eastern coast of North America just before the American Revolution. Despite great effort by the British parliament, the colonists were able to unite to fight British control over their developing settlements.

The First Continental Congress

On September 5, 1774, fifty-six delegates from twelve of the thirteen colonies met in Philadelphia, Pennsylvania. (Georgia did not send delegates, but vowed to support any decisions made by the Congress.) This meeting, the First Continental Congress, was attended by such patriots as George Washington, Samuel Adams, and John Hancock. The delegates were seeking fair treatment from England, not independence. The First Continental Congress was the earliest organized effort to liberate the colonies from British rule.

On October 14, 1774, the Congress adopted a Declaration of Rights and Grievances. This document stated that Parliament did not have the right to pass laws that affected America because the colonies had no representation in British government. It also claimed the right of each colony to regulate its own affairs.

Paper Work

Pretend that you were present at the First Continental Congress and helped draft the Declaration of Rights and Grievances.

✓ Write your own version of the Declaration of Rights and Grievances based on the information in the text above.

✓ Remember that the Congress was not seeking independence from England at this time, but rather equality.

✓ Think about the tone, or mood, you want to achieve as you write. How do you want the document to sound? Formal, informal, angry, pleading, apologetic? What results do you want the document to achieve?

The delegates of the Congress also set up the Continental Association. Under this organization, the colonies agreed not to conduct business with England until the British parliament amended its colonial taxation laws, particularly the Intolerable Acts. They sent the document to King George III, and agreed to meet again if he refused to address their grievances.

King George ignored the requests of the colonists and continued to build British forces in the colonies. Tensions between Parliament and the colonists continued to grow, neither side wanting to back down.

During the First Continental Congress, patriots decided to cut off all trade between the colonies and England until Parliament revoked the Intolerable Acts. Despite England's strong-arm tactics, the colonies worked together to weather economic losses that stemmed from their decision.

The American Revolutionary War

Tensions between British forces and patriot forces boiled over on April 19, 1775, in the towns of Lexington and Concord. The American Revolution had begun. On April 23, 1775, upon hearing of the initial confrontation, King George declared, "The colonies are in open and avowed rebellion. The die is now cast. The colonies must either submit or triumph."

Eight and a half years later, on September 3, 1783, the Treaty of Paris was signed, bringing the American Revolution to an end. The colonists won the war for independence. While the Boston Tea Party had been a relatively small event compared to those that followed, many historians consider it the first open act of unified

Q & A

Break the class into groups of four or five students each. Take turns discussing the following questions:

✓ Based on what you know about the Boston Tea Party, would you say that it was the direct cause of the American Revolution?

✓ If the Boston Tea Party had not occurred, do you think the American Revolution would not have happened?

✓ If the Boston Tea Party had not occurred, how do you think events would have been different?

In this print, American and British soldiers fight at close range during the Battle of Lexington in Massachusetts on April 19, 1775. The battle marked the beginning of the American Revolution.

defiance against the powerful British Empire. Had Samuel Adams and the Sons of Liberty not donned their Mohawk disguises and tossed the British tea into Boston Harbor, who knows what would have happened. Chances are, revolution would have eventually come about in another way. Today, however, we remember the Boston Tea Party as the "celebration" that led to the liberation of the American people and the formation of the United States of America.

Timeline

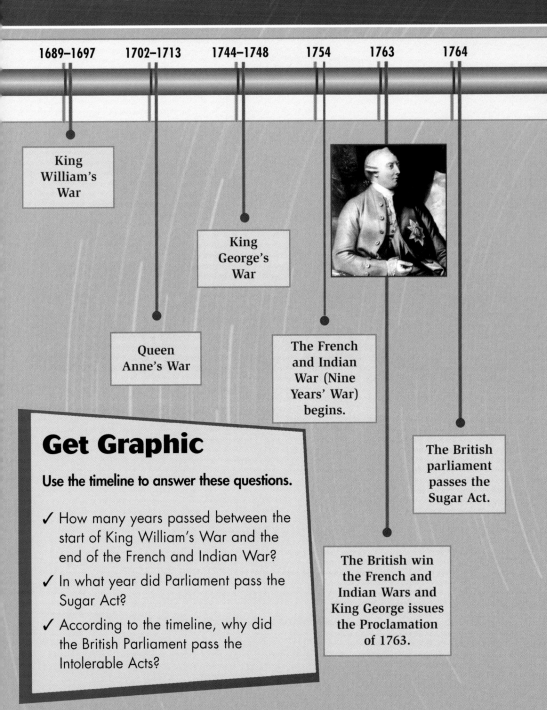

1689–1697   1702–1713   1744–1748   1754   1763   1764

King William's War

King George's War

Queen Anne's War

The French and Indian War (Nine Years' War) begins.

The British parliament passes the Sugar Act.

The British win the French and Indian Wars and King George issues the Proclamation of 1763.

Get Graphic

Use the timeline to answer these questions.

✓ How many years passed between the start of King William's War and the end of the French and Indian War?

✓ In what year did Parliament pass the Sugar Act?

✓ According to the timeline, why did the British Parliament pass the Intolerable Acts?

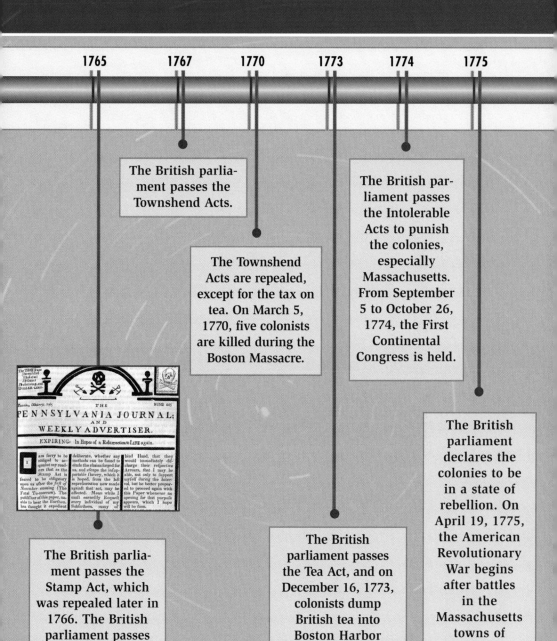

1765 **1767** **1770** **1773** **1774** **1775**

The British parliament passes the Townshend Acts.

The Townshend Acts are repealed, except for the tax on tea. On March 5, 1770, five colonists are killed during the Boston Massacre.

The British parliament passes the Intolerable Acts to punish the colonies, especially Massachusetts. From September 5 to October 26, 1774, the First Continental Congress is held.

The British parliament passes the Stamp Act, which was repealed later in 1766. The British parliament passes the Quartering Act.

The British parliament passes the Tea Act, and on December 16, 1773, colonists dump British tea into Boston Harbor causing the Boston Tea Party.

The British parliament declares the colonies to be in a state of rebellion. On April 19, 1775, the American Revolutionary War begins after battles in the Massachusetts towns of Lexington and Concord.

Graphic Organizers in Action

Get Graphic

Study the examples of graphic organizers on these pages.

✓ The series of events chain at right illustrates the events that led up to the Boston Massacre. Can you create a series of events chain that illustrates the events after the Boston Massacre that led to the Boston Tea Party?

✓ The Venn diagram below demonstrates the similarities and differences between patriots and Loyalists at the outbreak of the American Revolutionary War. Can you make a Venn diagram that illustrates the similarities and differences between the Boston Massacre and the Boston Tea Party?

Venn Diagram

Patriots

✓ Advocated independence from England
✓ Led protests against English taxes and control

✓ Lived in the British colonies
✓ Represented a large percentage of the total population of the colonies

Loyalists

✓ Advocated loyalty to England
✓ Were often British officers and representatives

In 1763, the British won the French and Indian Wars and gained control of nearly all of the French colonies in North America.

That same year, the British parliament passed the Proclamation of 1763, forbidding English colonists from settling on Indian lands.

The British parliament passed the Sugar Act (1764) and the Quartering Act (1765) to raise money to help pay off its war debt.

Colonists' protest of the Stamp Act often resulted in violence.

In 1765, the British parliament passed the Stamp Act to raise money and to assert its right to tax the colonists.

Colonists protested the Sugar and Quartering Acts.

The Stamp Act Congress of 1765 was the first united protest against the British.

In 1766, the British parliament repealed the Stamp Act and reduced the tax on molasses.

In 1767, the British parliament passed the Townshend Acts to raise money and to assert its right to tax the colonists.

On March 5, 1770, violence between colonists and British soldiers erupted in Boston, Massachusetts, resulting in the deaths of five colonists. Colonial advocates of American independence dubbed the event the Boston Massacre.

Colonial resentment over Parliament's insistence on its right to tax the colonies led to more frequent and violent protests.

Due to colonial protests, the British parliament repealed all of the Townshend Acts except for the duty on tea.

Glossary

alliance (uh-LYE-unz) A close association formed between people or groups of people to reach a common objective.

animosity (ahn-uh-MAH-sih-tee) Bad feelings between two parties that often results in fighting or violence.

coercive (koh-ER-siv) Restraining or dominating by force.

congress (KON-gres) A formal meeting of delegates.

customs (KUS-tums) Taxes or tolls placed on imports and exports.

encroach (in-KROHCH) To trespass on, or gradually take over, the property or rights of others.

intolerable (in-TOL-uh-ruh-bul) Unbearable.

massacre (MAH-sih-ker) The murder of a group of helpless people.

militia (muh-LIH-shuh) A group of people who are trained and ready to fight in an emergency.

monopoly (muh-NAH-puh-lee) Exclusive possession or control of a good or service.

oppress (uh-PRES) To govern harshly.

Parliament (PAR-luh-mint) The chief legislative body of some political systems. Specifically, the British legislative body, the House of Commons.

plunder (PLUN-der) To take by force.

proclamation (prah-kluh-MAY-shun) An official public announcement.

propaganda (prop-uh-GAN-duh) The spreading of information—whether true or false—for the purpose of helping or hurting an institution, person, or cause.

rebellion (ree-BEL-yun) Opposition to authority.

repeal (ree-PEEL) To cancel a previous act of legislation.

smuggle (SMUH-gul) To import or export secretly without paying duties imposed by law.

tyranny (TEER-uh-nee) Oppressive power wielded by a government.

Web Sites

Due to the changing nature of Internet links, the Rosen Publishing Group, Inc., has developed an online list of Web sites related to the subject of this book. This site is updated regularly. Please use this link to access the list:

http://www.rosenlinks.com/ctah/abtp

For Further Reading

Fradin, Dennis Brindell. *Samuel Adams: The Father of American Independence.* Boston, MA: Houghton Mifflin Company Trade & Reference Division, 1998.

Heinrichs, Ann. *Samuel Adams.* Eden Prairie, MN: The Child's World, Inc., 2004.

Hull, Mary E. *The Boston Tea Party in American History.* Berkeley Heights, NJ: Enslow Publishers, Inc., 1999.

Lukes, Bonnie L. *The Boston Massacre.* Farmington Hills, MI: The Gale Group, 1997.

Index

About the Author

Greg Roza has a bachelor's degree and a master's degree in English from the State University of New York at Fredonia. He has been writing history and science books with an emphasis on content tied directly to curriculum since 1999. He lives with his wife, Abigail, daughter, Autumn, and son, Lincoln, in upstate New York.

Photo Credits: Cover left, p. 29 © Poodles Rock/Corbis; cover right © Stock Montage/Getty Images; cover background, pp. 25, 40, 41 © National Archives and Records Administration, Washington, DC; pp. 5, 17, 19 © Bettmann/Corbis; pp. 9, 35 © Perry-Castañeda Library Map Collection/ Historical Maps of the Americas/The University of Texas at Austin; pp. 11, 31 © Hulton Archive/Getty Images; 13, 15, 33 © Bridgeman Art Library; p. 21 © Massachusetts Historical Society, Boston, MA/ Bridgeman Art Library; pp. 23, **39** © Corbis; p. 27 © Time Life Pictures/ Mansell/Getty Images; p. 37 © Atwater Kent Museum of Philadelphia/ Bridgeman Art Library.

Designer: Nelson Sá; Editor: Joann Jovinelly; Photo Researcher: Nelson Sá